CANNONBALL
SIMP

JOHN BURNINGHAM

CANDLEWICK PRESS
CAMBRIDGE, MASSACHUSETTS

for Acton

Second U.S. edition 1994
First published in 1966 by Jonathan Cape Ltd., London
by whose permission the present edition is published.

Library of Congress Cataloging-in-Publication Data

Burningham, John.
Cannonball Simp / written and illustrated by John Burningham.—2nd U.S. ed.
"First published in Great Britain in 1966"—T.p. verso.
Summary: A small dog, abandoned near a trash dump and captured
by a dog catcher, finds a home for herself when she is befriended
by a circus clown whose act needs improving.
ISBN 1-56402-338-9 (hardcover)—ISBN 1-56402-366-4 (pbk.)
[1. Dogs—Fiction.   2. Circus—Fiction.]   I. Title.
PZ7.B936Can   1994
[E]—dc20   93-32369

10 9 8 7 6 5 4 3 2 1

Printed in Belgium

The pictures in this book were done in ink and gouache.

Candlewick Press
2067 Massachusetts Avenue
Cambridge, Massachusetts 02140

Simp was what most people would call an ugly little dog. She was fat and small and had only a stump for a tail. Her owner had found homes for her brothers and sisters but could not persuade anybody to take Simp. So, in order to get rid of her, he decided to leave her somewhere, hoping that somebody would find her and take her in.

One evening he took Simp outside the town
and just left her near a garbage dump.

Poor little Simp watched the van disappearing into the distance. She could not understand why she had been left all alone. She did not know what to do. Then darkness fell. By the light of the moon she explored the dump and found an old armchair to spend the night in. Rats came out and looked curiously at her. When Simp said how hungry she was, one of them gave her a piece of bread. "But you'll have to go in the morning," he said. "It's hard enough for us rats to live. There wouldn't be enough food for you as well."

When it was light the next morning, Simp left the dump and wandered off in the direction of the town. She tried to make friends with people who were going to work, but nobody seemed to care about her. She spent a long time searching for something to eat, but she could not find anything.

Then she came across some trash cans. She started looking through them for food and did not notice the cats who were angrily watching her.

"That's my trash can," hissed one of the cats as he pounced. Simp ran for her life with the cat just behind her. She was running so fast that she did not look where she was going.

"Got you," said the dogcatcher. Two large hands grabbed Simp, and she was put in the back of the van with the other strays that the dogcatcher had collected. Almost all the other dogs in the van had homes. "We often get picked up," they said. "But what will become of you with no home to go to? And you don't even have a collar."

Simp became more and more worried as she talked to the other dogs. "Who can tell what may happen to you now?" one said. "You're not very pretty, are you?" said another. "I doubt if anybody will want to give you a home," said a third.

The van pulled into the yard of the dog pound. The doors were opened and the dogs driven toward the kennels. When the dogcatcher was looking the other way, Simp saw her chance. She jumped up on some boxes and was away over the wall.

Simp kept running and running until she was well out of town. Then, because she was still frightened, she crept into some thick bushes to hide. By the time it was dark she had become very hungry and set off again down the road.

Then, in the distance, Simp saw lights. They were the lights of a circus.

She went toward them, hoping she might find
someone there who would give her some food.

Perhaps after that she could curl up under
a trailer where it would be a little warmer.

She crept up to a trailer, climbed on a box, and
looked through the window. Inside was a clown
who was very surprised to see a little dog peering
at him. He opened the door and beckoned to Simp.
"You look very tired and hungry," said the clown,
and he gave Simp a large meal, which she gobbled
up. It was warm and comfortable in the trailer, and
the clown let Simp lie on his bed. She was soon
fast asleep.

The next morning the clown showed Simp
around the circus. There were many tents, trailers,
and animals. Simp met a young elephant and a lion.

Everybody seemed happy and friendly, but the clown was worried. People did not like his act anymore.

The clown told Simp exactly what he did. He showed her the cannon that fired a rubber ball through a paper hoop. Just then the ringmaster came up. "Unless you improve your act by tonight, you'll have to go," he said to the clown.

Simp had an idea. "That rubber ball is exactly the same size as me when I am curled up," she thought. "I just have time to work out a plan before the show starts."

The evening performance had begun. Just before the clown's act, Simp climbed into the cannon while nobody was looking. The man who was to fire the cannon peered inside and, seeing Simp curled up, thought she was the ball. Simp's heart was beating fast as she waited for the exciting moment to arrive.

The circus managers had a look of boredom on their faces as they watched the clown. "He'll really have to go," they said.

There was a rolling of drums and . . .

WHOOSH! Through the air flew Simp,
straight for the paper hoop. Right through
the hoop she went.

The crowds roared with delight when they saw
that the "cannonball" was a little black dog. The
clown was so surprised to see Simp that he almost
dropped the hoop.

Simp landed on a drum and stood there proudly while the audience cheered and cheered. She had really enjoyed being fired from the cannon. Then the clown and Simp were put on a horse and they went around and around the ring. Everybody was still wildly clapping and cheering.

After the show, the ringmaster gave a party for Simp and the clown. He invited the little elephant, the lion, and a monkey Simp had met, and they all ate until they were very full. The ringmaster told the clown and Simp that their act was the best the circus had ever had.

And so Simp lived happily with the clown
and traveled around the countryside with the
circus. The act became famous, and people came
especially to see the little dog fired from a cannon.
And that is how she came to be called
Cannonball Simp.

THE END

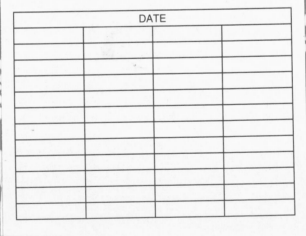

DATE			